DEDICATION

Gerald Red Elk, old friend and
former high school classmate

ACKNOWLEDGEMENTS

I am grateful for the constant support of my wife, Tina, and my children, Jacob, Caleb, Sarah and Ainslee.

Thank you to Missy Brewer for editing this book, to Michael Campbell for the book design, and to Bryan Gehrke for the cover artwork.

John 14:6 Jesus answered, "I am the way and the truth and the life. No one comes to the Father except through me."

THE LAST OF THE

THE LEGEND OF JAKE JACKSON

GREAT GUNFIGHTERS

BOOK FIVE

A WESTERN ADVENTURE

WILLIAM H. JOINER JR.

Copyright © 2019 by William H. Joiner Jr.

Published by DS Productions

ISBN: 9781674383743

A NOTE FROM
BESTSELLING AUTHOR
ROBERT HANLON

Those who have had the pleasure of reading the great Westerns Bill Joiner writes—yes I know—many of you already know what I am going to say. Those who have had the pleasure—well let me just cut it short and tell you that he has a great style you'll love. Joiner, to me, is one of those writers who can really get a story across to his audience. He has drive. He's a driven writer—and you'll love this one. It's called "The Legend of Jake Jackson" and it's the kind-of story you've been asking for. Action, gunplay and lots of story. Grab it!

*Robert Hanlon – author of the bestselling "*Timber: United States Marshal*" series, and many other Western adventures.*

A NOTE FROM
BESTSELLING AUTHOR
JOHN D. FIE, JR.

Well... what can I say other than give this one a shot! It's the latest, and greatest from the talented Mister Joiner.

Jake Jackson's real family gets killed by a warring Indian party. He is raised by the Indians and becomes a celebrated warrior. Disaster strikes when the Comanche are moved to a reservation. I won't tell you the rest—but our hero becomes mighty good with a gun.

Heck—forget my blathering! Just read the book!

John D. Fie, Jr. – author of the bestselling "Gunfighter" series, and many other Western adventures.

"Jake Jackson was a legend in the Old West. His ability with a gun was unmatched. His name brought hope to the oppressed and sent shivers of fear up the spines of outlaws. Jake Jackson was equally as revered among the Comanche where he was raised from an infant to become the Comanche Warrior, White Wolf. There were many songs sung around campfires in Comanche villages praising his fierceness in battle.

Jake Jackson could revert back to his Comanche ways in the blink of an eye when the situation demanded no mercy to those preying on the weak or unprotected."

Jake no longer had the wanderlust. He preferred staying home with his wife Anne, their son Caleb Burk and Burk Burnett. Burk Burnett thought of Jake, Anne and Caleb Burk as his family. Nothing made him happier than when Anne called him Pa and Caleb Burk addressed him as Grandpa. Caleb Burk had recently turned 12 years old. Burk had been thrilled when Jake and Anne named their son after him.

Jake ramrodded the Four-Sixes for Burnett. The ranch was the largest in north Texas. Burk had long said that the Jacksons were going to inherit the ranch. Neither Jake nor Anne cared a whit about owning the ranch. Their love for Burk had nothing to do with property or things.

Rumors had circulated for years that Jake was dead. People always like to gossip. It seemed like the less the truth, the more the gossip. A cowboy stopped Burk in town, "Excuse me, sir. I heared somebody said that you was kin to Jake Jackson. I keep hearing that he's dead. If you don't mind me asking, is that true?"

Burk snorted, "Unless he died in the last hour, Jake was in perfect health when I left him. Anybody who thinks any different is welcome to tie into him. I reckon they'll find he still has the bark on him!" The cowboy grinned, "That's good to hear! We've lost too many great men as it is. Glad to know Mr. Jackson is still kicking!"

Albert Gordon was one of 13 children born to John and Millie Gordon. John was a sharecropper in Tallapoosa County, Alabama. John was worried, "Millie, the weevils got most of the cotton this year. Mr. Cagle was supposed to sell what we harvested yesterday. I gotta go see him today for our share of the money. I got a knot in the pit of my stomach. I'm afraid it won't be much."

Eli Cagle saw John come up the driveway. He stepped out on the porch to meet him. John stood at the bottom of the porch steps with his hat in his hand. John nodded, "Good morning, Mr. Cagle. It's a fine day, ain't it?" Eli snapped, "John, I'm going to get right to it. I never seen prices this low for cotton. And on top of that we had damn little of it to sell. I'm taking a loss on your cotton crop this year. I ain't got no money for you."

It took a minute for John to understand, "There's no money? Surely, Mr. Cagle, there's got to be something! I got 13 kids. I can't make it with no money!" Eli retorted, "That ain't my problem. Nobody told you to have them passel of kids! That's your own doing!" John replied, "But..." Eli interrupted, "There ain't no buts to it. There's no money! Go on before I sic my dogs on you!"

That night over their usual cornbread supper, John made an announcement. Most of the children knew something was wrong because their Ma had been crying during supper. John said, "I ain't never seen times as hard as they is now. We got no money from our cotton this year. We got to do some hard things. The oldest seven boys are going to have to leave and make your own way in the world. Me and Ma are going to try to take care of the girls and the young'uns."

Albert asked, "Even me, Pa?" That made Millie cry harder. John nodded, "Yes, son. I know you're only 12, but you're big for your age. You're a hard worker. You'll make it."

The next morning amid much weeping, John and Mille sent the seven boys out into the world. There was no money, but each boy carried a sack of corn dodgers. The boys tried to stay together. On the second day on the trail headed west, the boys were ambushed by a gang of outlaws. When the gunsmoke cleared, all of Albert's brothers had been shot to death. All except Albert. In all the commotion, Albert managed to dive off into a dry creek bed. He hid among the roots of an old tree.

Albert heard one of the outlaws shout, "Well, I'll be a sum bitch! These farmboys ain't got nothing, but corn dodgers! What a waste of good bullets!" Albert waited most of the day before crawling out. He fearfully checked the bloodied bodies of his brothers for signs of life to no avail. They were all dead.

Albert sat cross-legged with his head in his hands. He cried harder than he ever had in his entire life. Within 24 hours Albert no longer recognized his world that he used to live in. Finally, he murmured, "Boys, I ain't got no shovel to bury y'all. I hope you won't hold it agin me." Albert briefly thought about going back home. He decided against it. Albert announced to his dead brothers, "I reckon I'll be going on west. I don't want to be no burden to Ma and Pa."

That night Albert saw a glimmer of a campfire through the trees. He slowly crept toward the light. Butch and Leroy were two saddle tramps who stole and cheated to get the money for the rot-gut they both lived for. Butch laughed, "Pass me that bottle, damn you! You're keeping it too long. You're drinking your whiskey and mine too."

Dan who was tied to a tree outside of the light from the campfire, spotted Albert. The old mule brayed a warning. Leroy declared, "I see him too, Dan!" He pulled his pistol, "Come out where I can see you better or I'm gonna blast you!" Albert timidly stepped into the firelight. Butch exclaimed, "It's just a durn kid!" Leroy

3

added, "A mighty fine looking one too." Butch cast a disproving look to Leroy, "Put down your gun."

Butch asked, "What are you doing, boy?" Albert's teeth chattered, "I was hoping I could warm up by your fire." Butch grinned, "Sure, help yourself!" Leroy asked, "Why are you alone? You are alone, ain't you?" Albert replied, "My folks are going through hard times. I figured it was time I got out on my own...earn my own way."

Later that night Leroy offered, "I'll share my blanket with you, Albert. Be good for both of us on a cold night like tonight." That didn't bother Albert any. He was used to sleeping with his brothers back home. An exhausted Albert quickly drifted off to sleep. Albert woke up because Leroy was tugging on his britches. Albert began to struggle and fight. Leroy whispered, "Dammit boy, hold still." Leroy clamped a hand over Albert's mouth to keep him from crying out. As Albert thrashed around his hand came in contact with Leroy's gun. John had showed all his children how to fire an old pistol that he had. Albert managed to wrestle the gun out of its holster. Albert had only wanted to scare Leroy into leaving him alone.

Albert managed to cock the sixgun just as Leroy rolled over on top of him. The pistol fired. A startled look came on Leroy's face before his eyes lost their sight. Albert squirmed out from under Leroy's body. Butch jumped up at the sound of the gunfire. Butch exclaimed, "What in tarnation?" He threw back the blanket, "You ungrateful whelp! You kilt Leroy!"

Butch took a step towards Albert. In what would seem like a dream afterwards, Albert cocked and triggered the pistol again. Butch staggered at the blow from the slug. He put his hands over the bullet hole hoping to stop the bleeding. Butch teetered for a moment before toppling over backwards. He landed in the fire, scattering sparks.

Albert didn't sleep the rest of the night. He kept the gun at the ready, pointed at the bodies. Albert wasn't convinced that the dead men were really dead.

At dawn Albert dragged the bodies into a nearby ditch. He tried to cover them with branches and rocks as best he could. When he finished, he proclaimed over the make-shift grave, "Reckon y'all got what you deserved." Albert went through Butch's and Leroy's possessions. He put everything he thought he could use in Dan's pack. Albert had increased his poke with food, clothes, guns and two $5 gold pieces. He patted the mule on the shoulder, "I guess it's you and me now, Dan."

Since Leroy was a small man, Albert changed into his extra clothes, hat and boots. He also strapped on Leroy's holstered pistol. Every couple of days, Albert took target practice with the sixgun. He became confident that he could hit what he was aiming at.

When Albert ran out of food, he stopped at a mercantile in a small town in Louisiana. As he was carrying the foodstuffs outside, Albert noticed there was a man standing by Dan. Albert began loading the food into Dan's pack. The stranger remarked, "Hey kid, ain't that ol' Dan? Used to belong to Butch? How'd you come by him?"

Albert replied, "Found him running loose over in Alabama. I didn't see no owner so I gave him a home." The stranger scratched his beard, "That just don't figure. Butch set great store on that mule. I don't see Butch letting him wander off unless something happened to Butch." Albert responded, "I don't know nothing about that."

Albert untied Dan and started to lead him away. The stranger grabbed Albert's arm, "Boy, don't you be turning your back on me! Besides, I got me a sneaking suspicion that you know more than what you're letting on!" Albert jerked his arm away, "Mister, leave me be!" The stranger began to pull his gun, "I done told you..." Albert dropped the lead rope. He drew his pistol and fired all in one smooth motion.

The blast from the bullet knocked the stranger to the ground. The stranger stared incredulously at the blood pouring from the hole in his chest. The town constable heard the shot. He ran up with his gun drawn, "What happened here?" One of the bystanders declared, "It was self-defense! I seen it all. The kid was just trying to defend himself!" A second observer confirmed it, "Yep, I seen it too! The man on the ground drew first!"

The Constable asked Albert, "What's your name, boy? Where you from? What's your business here?" Albert replied, "I'm Albert Gordon from Alabama. I'm passing through on my way to Texas." The Constable responded, "Well, Albert Gordon from Alabama, I don't like no trouble in my town. I suggest you be on your way to Texas." Albert smiled, "Yes, sir. I plan on doing just that."

Later Albert shook his head in amazement. He asked Dan, "What do you reckon Pa would say if he knowed I killed three men?" Dan just kept following Albert. Albert continued, "I ain't had no choice. It was them or me. I don't think Pa would like it none, but I bet he would understand."

It wasn't long after Albert crossed over into Texas when gun blasts rang out. Bullets were buzzing by Albert's head. Albert dove off into the cover of some shinnery. As he searched for the source of the attack,

Albert saw to his horror that Dan had been shot. The mule was lying on his side with a bullet wound bubbling air from a lung. Dan was struggling to breathe.

A voice from behind a grove of pine trees exclaimed, "I think we got him!" Another voice replied, "Go check!" One of the outlaws crept out of hiding with his gun drawn. Albert held his breath as the man got closer. The outlaw exclaimed, "I don't see the ol' boy that was leading the mule, but the mule's done for!"

The anger at Dan being killed welled up in Albert. He pulled the trigger on his cocked gun. The .45 slug tunneled a hole in the outlaw's belly. The bandit screamed as he dropped to his knees, "I've been shot!" Albert was laying three feet from the wounded killer. Albert whispered, "Get the rest of them out here or the next bullet will be between your eyes." Albert was no longer a boy. He thought and acted like a man.

Baxter clutched his stomach. He desperately shouted, "Gil...Jim! Get over here! I need your help!" Gil responded, "Where's the one who shot you?" Baxter answered, "He done skedaddled! Help me! I'm dying!" Gil and Jim cautiously approached their pard. Albert shot Gil in the leg. The next bullet almost took off Jim's head. Gil yelled, "Baxter, you double-crossing polecat!" Gil plugged Baxter in the back before passing out.

When Gil regained consciousness, he was lying between his former partners. Gil looked up to see the muzzle of Albert's Colt pointed at him. Gil begged, "Now take it easy, mister. I didn't mean no harm. It was the other two who made me do this. I was raised going to church. It's agin my Christian upbringing to hurt someone. If you let me go, I'll swear I'll never do nothing like this again!"

It had hurt Albert to see the dead bodies of his brothers. For some reason the hurt was even greater with Dan's death. Albert's humanity died with the mule. Albert carefully aimed his pistol, "Shut your lying mouth!" The bullet crashed through the teeth of Gil's open mouth. His head bucked from the force of the slug.

The gang of renegades had three horses, two branded, one unbranded. Albert unsaddled and turned the branded ones loose. He put the best saddle on the remaining horse. He stroked the horse's mane, "If you ain't got no objections, I'm gonna call you Dan. I once had me a good friend by the name of Dan."

Albert had changed drastically. He had killed six men and he wouldn't turn 13 years old until next month. His Pa had been right about one thing. Albert was big for his age. His boyish features revealed a boy who had been jerked by life's circumstances into manhood.

When Albert arrived in Ft. Worth, he started to frequent saloons and acquired a taste for whisky. Hard drinking impacted his childlike face. Albert began to look older than he actually was.

Fred who was the bartender at the White Elephant, kept his hand on the shot glass, "Where's the money, Albert? I can't let you drink on the dole. Everybody pays cash." Albert blinked in his drunken stupor, "Okay, Fred. Whatever you say." Albert stumbled out of the door. He passed out in the alley behind the saloon.

When Albert came to, he was lying next to another drunk who was sleeping it off. Despite the man's loud snoring, when Albert reached inside the drunk's coat pocket for cash, he grabbed Albert's wrist in a vise-like grip. The drunk snorted, "Oh no you don't, feller! I can't abide no thief." The drunk began to yell, "Sheriff!..."

Albert struck the man over the head with the barrel of his gun to shut him up. The drunk loosened his grip on Albert's wrist but managed to hold on.

As the drunk continued to struggle, Albert hit him two more times with his gun. Blood gushed from the huge gash in his victim's head. Albert pulled money out of his pocket and hurried back into the saloon. Albert leaned against the bar. He slapped the cash on the bar as he ordered, "Gimme a whisky, Fred! I found me some money."

An hour later, a cowboy rushed through the batwing doors. He shouted, "They just found old Jonah out back! He's dead! Someone bashed his head in!" Fred looked at the flecks of blood on Albert's sleeve. The bartender sighed. He learned a long time ago that it was best to mind his own business. Fred kept his opinions to himself.

One day Lee Martin sat down at the same table as Albert. Albert glanced up from his drink, "Can I help you?" Lee smiled, "Maybe...Maybe we can help each other." Albert replied, "I'm busy. Go away." Lee responded, "Too busy to make a thousand dollars?" Albert arched his eyebrows, "Doing what?"

Lee waved at the bartender, "Hey Fred, bring us another round." Lee looked at Albert, "On me!" Albert eyeballed the man closely for the first time, "Okay, you've got my attention...What's the deal on the thousand dollars?"

Lee waited for the rot-gut to be delivered before continuing, "I've seen you around for a while and unless I miss my guess, you're what I'm looking for in a partner. You just have that look about you. A man not to be trifled with. A man who can and will do what it takes. A man who if the going gets tough, won't bail on a partner."

Albert smirked, "You can tell all that by just looking?...How much have you had to drink?" Lee laughed, "You might be surprised at how good a judge of people I am."

Lee leaned in to speak in a low voice, "I had me a pretty good deal going when my partner got a little greedy. He left me no choice but to...terminate our partnership. The deal I got is a bird's nest on the ground. We steal a few cattle. I got a buyer in west Texas who pays cash on the barrelhead for every cow I bring him. I need a partner who's got the sand to ride the river with me...And don't get too greedy. I get 75% for setting everything up. You get 25% for helping me out."

Albert mulled the offer for a minute, "How do I know this will work like you say?" Lee shrugged, "How much money you making now?" Albert grinned, "Howdy, partner."

Lee and Albert had watched the old man tend his small herd south of San Angelo for several days. He had no cowboys, just an old woman at the shanty that passed as a ranch house. They assumed she was his wife.

Lee chortled, "Ahh, this is perfect. Me and you can easily take the cows and drive them to west Texas for a payday!" Albert asked, "What do you want to do about the old man and old woman?" Lee retorted, "What do you think I want to do about them? No witnesses! You might as well get your mind right. You won't last in this business by leaving witnesses! I ain't letting nobody live that might put my neck in a noose!...I thought we done talked about this. You having second thoughts?" Albert spit, "Hell no! Just wanted to make sure how we was going to handle this!"

Mary kissed Bob just like she did every morning before he rode out to see about the cattle. Mary winked, "You be careful. I need you back here tonight." They had been married over 40 years, but their love affair was still strong.

Bob was surprised when the two men rode out of a mesquite thicket with their guns drawn. Bob exclaimed, "What the hell do you saddle tramps want?" Lee smirked, "Not a whole lot, old timer. We just want to borrow them cows for a spell." Bob's hand went for the butt of his Colt, "I'll send you to hell first!" Lee and Albert fired at the same time. The twin blasts jarred Bob from his saddle. Bob Cook was dead before he hit the prairie.

Mary's heart fluttered when she saw Bob's horse gallop up without Bob. She grabbed the double-barrel shotgun that was propped in the corner. Her knuckles were white as Mary tightly gripped the old gun. Her worst fears were confirmed when two riders approached the house.

One of the men shouted, "Hello, the house! You man's been hurt! He sent us to fetch you. He needs your help!" Mary poked the barrel of the shotgun out of in the crack in the door, "What's wrong with him?" Lee responded, "His horse must have stepped in a hole and threw the old feller. He's banged up pretty bad!"

Every sense told Mary that something was wrong. Still with any chance that Bob might need her, she lowered the shotgun and stepped out on the porch. Albert had maneuvered his horse behind Lee's to conceal his drawn pistol. When Mary exposed herself, Albert spurred his horse forward a step and triggered his gun.

The .45 slug struck Mary in the chest, slamming her back against the door. Lee crowed, "Good shot, partner! I knowed you had it in you!" Both killers watched as Mary slumped over in a pool of her own blood.

Burk jumped up from the rocker on the porch at the big house on the Four-Sixes ranch. He grinned at the incoming rider, "Well, bless my soul if it ain't Buzzard Wells! Get down off that horse, you old cow thief! I figured they hung you a long time ago!"

Buzzard shook Burk's extended hand before they bear-hugged, slapping each other on the back. Anne smiled as she watched the old friends greet each other. Buzzard asked, "How long has it been, Burk?" Burk scratched his head, "I reckon it's been nigh on to 30 years!" Buzzard replied, "It seems like just yesterday that we was cowboying together." Burk nodded, "You got that right, pard. Time gets away from me."

Burk gestured to Anne, "Buzzard, I want you to meet my daughter, Anne...Anne, me and Buzzard Wells go back a long way." Buzzard tipped his hat, "Pleasure to meet you, ma'am." Burk pulled up another chair, "Sit down, Buzzard and rest your old carcass...Tell me what you been doing for the last 30 years." Anne smiled at Buzzard.

Buzzard wearily sat down. He sighed, "Mainly drifting from ranch to ranch working cattle. I wished I had the sense to stay hooked with you. I'd been a whole lot better off." Burk smiled, "Well, you're here now. What caused you to look me up after all these years?" Buzzard frowned, "After attending Bob's funeral, I got to thinking that all my old pards was dying off. I figured if I wanted to see any of them again, I needed to get to getting."

It took a moment for what Buzzard said to sink in, Burk replied, "Bob's funeral? You don't mean Bob Cook, do you?" Buzzard sadly responded, "They buried him and

Mary both. I don't know if you knew Bob got hitched." Burk stated, "I think I heard something about Bob getting married, but I never met her…What happened?" Anger flashed in Buzzard's eyes, "Two sum bitches murdered them!" Buzzard nodded to Anne, "Sorry, ma'am, bout my language." Anne replied, "No apologies needed, Mr. Wells. Sounds like to me that the killers were sum bitches."

Buzzard muttered, "If it had been 10 years ago, them boys wouldn't be breathing right now! These days I got me a slip in my get-a-long that keeps me from doing what I used to do." Anne announced, "Mr. Wells, I insist you stay for supper." Burk slapped his knee, "Of course, you're staying for supper. You'll get to meet my son, Jake Jackson and my grandson, Caleb Burk…They named him after me!"

Buzzard paused, "Wait a minute…Jake Jackson, the famous gunfighter? He's your son?" Burk grinned, "Well, maybe by blood he ain't, but I claim him as my son. That seems to be agreeable to him." As the men continued to talk, Anne thought, "I don't want Jake to hear this story about those poor folks who got murdered. He's going to want to go after the killers. I hate it when he's gone."

Jake and Caleb Burk rode in at sundown. Caleb Burk was now 12 and spent most days with his Pa looking after the ranch. After they rubbed down and fed their horses at the barn, father and son went to the big house for supper.

Jake had noticed the strange horse in the corral so he wasn't surprised when Burk said, "Jake, I want you to meet an old pard of mine, Buzzard Wells." Jake shook his hand, "Burk tells some stories about you and him back in the day. It's good to finally meet you…This is my son,

Caleb Burk." Caleb Burk stepped up and gave Buzzard a firm handshake. Burk beamed, "They named him after me." Buzzard grinned, "So I heard."

Burk prodded Buzzard into telling Jake about the murder of Bob and Mary Cook. Jake asked, "The law can't find the killers?" Buzzard snorted, "The law south of San Angelo couldn't find a stagecoach in a bank lobby!" Burk never said anything else, but he kept looking sideways at Jake.

After they finished supper, everyone retired to the cool breeze on the porch. Finally, Jake shrugged, "I reckon I might ride down there in the morning to see what I can see." Buzzard replied, "Jake, it's been over two weeks. We had a couple of hard rains. I speck the trail is cold." Burk bragged, "That don't make my boy no nevermind. He was raised by the Comanche, you know. Jake can track a snake over a rock slide!"

Anne never said a word about the pending trip. She knew that once Jake got something set in his mind, that was it. There was no stopping him. That was a trait in Jake's personality that Anne loved and hated at the same time. Caleb Burk pleaded, "Pa, ain't I big enough to go with you now. You said yourself the other day how I could already ride and shoot like a grown man." Anne breathed a sigh of relief when Jake replied, "Not quite, son, but you're getting there. Besides I need you to watch out for your Ma and Grandpa." Burk muttered under his breath, "I don't need no damn protecting." Burk didn't say it out loud because he didn't want to hurt Caleb Burk's feelings.

Jake left at first light. Caleb Burk had already saddled Buck and tied him to the hitching rail in front of the house. Jake hugged and kissed Anne. He shook hands with Burk and Buzzard who had decided to stay a few days at Burk's urging.

Jake smiled when Caleb Burk thrust out his hand for a handshake instead of being hugged by his Pa. His boy was in a hurry to grow up. Jake said, "You did a mighty fine job of saddling Buck. No man could have done it better." Caleb Burk glowed under the praise from his Pa. He lived for Jake's approval. The only ones that Buck would allow touching him besides Jake were Anne and Caleb Burk. Any other man put his life at risk by trying to put a hand on the horse.

Burk found that out the hard way when he tried to catch Buck in the corral. Buck mule-kicked at Burk and chased him out of the pen, snapping his teeth. Burk swore, "If that damn horse was mine, I'd feed him to the coyotes!"

Jake didn't go all the way to San Angelo. He figured the rustlers could only go two places, either Mexico or west Texas. Jake told Buck, "I don't figure Mexico, too far. More likely west Texas." Jake cut cross country. He intercepted the tracks of the cattle just east of the Davis Mountains. As it turned out he was only two days behind the slow-moving herd.

Jake followed the tracks onto the Bar X ranch. He asked one of the ranch hands, "Where can I find the ramrod of this outfit?" The surly cowboy snarled, "We ain't hiring! Specially not no saddle tramps!" Jake rode up close enough to grab the front of the cowhand's shirt. Jake jerked him off his horse and over Buck's neck. Jake pushed the point of his knife against the cowboy's throat hard enough that the blood began to trickle. Jake exclaimed, "I'm going to ask you just one more time. If I don't like the answer, I might get a little rough with you,

"Where is your ramrod?" The cowboy croaked, "He's two miles south of here in the next pasture." Jake let him go. The cowhand hit the ground with a thud and a small puff of dust.

Jake quietly rode up to three cowboys branding cows. He noticed they were putting a new brand over an old brand. Jake exclaimed, "You boys look like you're pretty good with that running iron!" All three cowboys dropped what they were doing and put the hands on the butts of their pistols. One demanded, "What business is it of yours? You ain't even supposed to be on the Bar X! Nobody is except them that are riding for the brand! You need to get and don't never come back!"

Jake grinned, "Mister, that ain't very friendly. If y'all pull those hog-legs, I'll have to kill you. I wouldn't like that. I'm damn sure you wouldn't like it!" The talker snorted, "Them's big words for one gun agin three! Boys, let's learn this loud mouth!"

The talker didn't get his gun moved more than an inch before a .45 slug from Jake's Colt tore out his throat. The second thief took a bullet in the right eye. The third one was shot through his left eye. The three bodies were crumpled together, staining the ground with blood, brain parts and pieces of skull.

It had been awhile since Jake had been in a gunfight. He chose different spots on each man to sharpen himself to a keen edge.

Jake had dropped the reins on Buck right before the shooting started. Despite the barrage of bullets, Buck munched on the tender grass without so much as a flicker of an ear. Buck bowed his neck to look back at Jake. His look seem to say, "Keep on shooting. I'm kinda busy here."

Jake back trailed the three dead men, attempting to locate the headquarters of the Bar X. He saw plenty of cattle wearing the Bar X brand, some with another brand underneath that only an experienced cattleman would have noticed.

Finally Jake spotted a handful of buildings on the horizon. He rode up to the house, barn and bunkhouse. There were almost a dozen pens. One of the men with a foot on the bottom rung of the biggest pen exclaimed, "Mister, you're trespassing! Get the hell off the Bar X or we'll bury you here!"

Jake chuckled, "That's just like a damn Apache. Always making noise when they should shut up." The half-breed was startled, "Who says I'm an Apache?" Jake grinned, "I do. I'm Comanche. I can smell the stink of an Apache at a half-mile!"

A second man interjected, "Shut up, Mingo! I'll do the talking around here." He turned to Jake, "State your business! And be quick about it!" Jake's eyes narrowed, "I'm looking for two rustlers. Brought in a herd yesterday from south of San Angelo. The man they stole the cows from is a friend of mine. I'm here to settle up."

Six hands of the Bar X had gathered around. They appeared to be spoiling for a fight, especially Mingo. The man declared, "I'm Sam Hunter. I run this outfit for Mr. James Fairfield of Denver, Colorado. I say who settles what on Bar X land! You act like you're wanting a quick burial! We can durn sure accommodate you!"

Jake laughed, "Since you're in a burying mood, I left three of your bunch lying in a nice neat pile. They were working a running iron on some stolen cows. You should be able to get them in the ground without too much fuss. Getting me in the ground might be a tad harder chore."

This time Jake took the fight to them. He didn't wait for them to make the first move. Jake jerked his pistol and fanned the hammer. The first bullet blew off the ramrod's hat with a piece of his skull in it. The second slug pounded Mingo in the belly. He fell to his knees trying to hold his guts in his stomach. The next two gang members turned tail and ran. As they mounted their saddled horses and rode off, one of them exclaimed, "I thought I recognized that ol' boy. After seeing him shoot, I'm sure of it. That was Jake Jackson!"

There were two outlaws left. One had fumbled his gun and dropped it in the dirt. The other had thrust both hands in the air and begged, "Please, mister, don't shoot! Let me ride away and I won't bother you no more!" Jake asked, "If the two of you want to live, I want some information. Then I want you to ride for Mexico and don't come back!" The man replied, "Whatever you say! I'll ride for the border. I'll get me a senorita and won't ever come back." The other man was vigorously nodding his head in agreement.

Jake continued, "I want to know who the men were that brought that herd in yesterday? I want to know where they went?" The outlaw replied, "One was called Albert. The other was Lee. They left here headed north. I swear that's all I know!" Jake motioned south with his sixgun, "Skedaddle!" The former ranch hands left the Bar X at a full gallop.

Jake set fire to the house, barn and bunkhouse. As he watched it burn, Jake told Buck, "Mr. James Fairfield of Denver, Colorado has got some work to do to get back in business!...Speaking of business, we still got some to tend to."

Lee and Albert set up camp in the Davis Mountains. They fried up bacon for their supper. When the embers of their fire started to die down, Lee thumbed through the money, "A thousand dollars! Not bad for a few weeks work!" Albert gulped the last of their whiskey. He chunked the empty bottle into the fire. Albert responded, "I felt a little bad about shooting that old woman even though I knew it had to be done. Seeing that money makes me feel better."

Albert laid back on his blanket resting his head on his saddle, "Lee, how many of these jobs do you think we could do in a year?" Lee shrugged, "I ain't for certain, but it should be a bunch. Enough for us to get rich and live in a fancy hotel with all the whiskey and women we want." Albert grinned, "I'm glad I threw in with you. It's good to know we'll be getting what we deserve!"

A loud voice woke the miscreants from their drunken stupor the next morning. The voice inquired, "You pilgrims going to sleep the day away? Ain't you worried that you might miss out on slaughtering another old man and old woman for their property?"

Lee and Albert leapt to their feet, shucking their blankets. They both had their guns out scanning their surroundings. Lee demanded, "Who are you? Come out where I can see you!" Just then a mule deer who had been watching the scene, bolted through the trees. Albert emptied his gun at the commotion.

Jake laughed as he stepped out in the open, "A little jumpy, ain't you?" Albert hurriedly began to reload his gun. Jake grinned, "You can go to all that trouble to reload your shooter, but you aren't going to live long enough to need all those bullets."

Lee began to sweat and his gun hand trembled, "I don't know who you are, but I can shut you up by pulling this trigger. You might be some kinda fast gunslinger, but nobody's that fast!" Jake responded, "I don't normally talk this much. When you get to Hell, tell the Devil that Jake Jackson sent you."

Jake's hand was a blur that most humans could not see. He pulled and shot his Colt before Lee could put enough pressure on the trigger to fire his gun. The slug slammed into Lee's chest, dropping him to his knees. As the life drained from his eyes, Lee managed to mutter, "I ain't never..."

When Lee's lifeless body toppled over, Albert threw down his gun. Albert exclaimed, "I'm done, Mr. Jackson! I give up! Take me to jail! I know when I'm whooped!" Jake declared, "I ain't taking you anywhere. You've murdered and robbed innocent folks. Justice is going to be done right here." Albert pleaded, "Please, please..." The .45 bullet from Jake's gun silenced Albert's begging. The slug entered the bridge of Albert's nose, slinging blood and shards of bone over Lee's body.

Jake mounted Buck, "I guess the coyotes and buzzards will eat good today...C'mon, boy, let's go home."

Caleb Burk had inherited Jake's keen eyesight. He shouted, "It's Pa! Pa's coming!" Caleb Burk was waiting to take Buck's reins to lead him to the barn to be fed and watered. Caleb Burk asked, "Did you get em, Pa? Did you get em?" Jake smiled, "I got em, son."

Anne ran down the steps, threw her arms around Jake's neck. As she kissed him, she whispered, "I am so glad you're back." Jake replied, "Not any gladder than me to be back."

Burk stated, "It's about time you came home. You know a ranch like this doesn't run itself!" Jake laughed, "It's good to see you too, Burk."

Frank Stillwell celebrated his election as the new sheriff of Marfa at the Yellow Dog Saloon with some of his cronies who helped rig the election. Stillwell was the front man for J.B. Booker who was the president of the only bank in town, Farmers and Ranchers Savings. The relationship between Stillwell and Booker was the worst kept secret in Presidio County. Most folks knew they were shady, but no one wanted to sign their own death warrant by trying to prove it.

Booker had publicly endorsed Stillwell, "Frank Stillwell will make as fine a sheriff as Texas has ever seen. Mr. Stillwell is a man of integrity and honesty. The citizens of Marfa will be in good hands with Frank Stillwell as sheriff." It was rumored that there might be another couple of candidates considering running for sheriff. Their aspirations were doused after a visit from Stillwell and his henchmen.

Booker liked to boast, "There's not a dollar that changes hands in Presidio County that I don't get a piece of. You want to buy something, give me my two bits." Stillwell was the perfect stooge for Booker. Stillwell had no conscious. As long as Booker paid him, he did what he was told.

Ernest Canton sat across the spacious desk from J.B. Booker. Ernest nervously twisted his hat in his hands. He explained, "So you see, Mr. Booker, I've just had a run of bad luck. I remember you said when I took out the loan on my place that if I ever had a problem paying the bank, just come see you...I need the bank to give me more time."

Booker strummed his fingers on his desk. He stared off into space as if he was in deep thought. Booker counted on this day coming. He knew exactly what he would do the day Ernest signed the loan agreement on his ranch.

Booker gave a fake sigh. With a raised eyebrow, Booker shook his head, "Mr. Canton, I'm afraid there's not any way I can give you an extension on your note. If I did something that reckless, the stockholders of the bank would be calling for my job." Ernest began to panic, "But, Mr. Booker, without that extension I'll lose everything! Me and Abby won't have a home! What will we do?"

Booker shrugged, "I wish I could help. I surely do. I just can't." Ernest jumped up from his chair. He was livid. Ernest shouted, "Can't or won't! I don't believe there's any stockholders! You own the bank! You could give me that extension! You're trying to steal my place! I know you've always had an eye on it. You want it because of the water! I'm hiring me a lawyer. We'll see what a federal judge has to say about it!"

After Ernest stormed out of the bank, Booker sent for Stillwell, "Frank, Ernest Canton is giving me a problem. I don't want to go through a delay of a lawsuit. I need that place now. That spring-fed creek is as good as gold. Take care of it."

Stillwell and three of his deputies rode up to the ranch house. Ernest had seen them coming. He was standing on the porch with a double-barrel shotgun nestled in the crook of his arm. Ernest demanded, "Get off my property, Stillwell! You and your drinking buddies got no business here!"

Stillwell smiled, "Now Canton, that ain't no way to talk to the Sheriff. That might make me think you and me ain't friends. I wouldn't like that. I wouldn't like that atall." Without warning Stillwell drew his pistol and shot Ernest. The force of the bullet striking his chest caused Ernest to drop his shotgun. Ernest hit the porch on his back causing a small puff of dust.

As blood flowed from the bullet hole, Abby shrieked, "Ernest! Ernest!" She cradled her dying husband's head in her lap. Abby sobbed uncontrollably. One of the deputies reminded Stillwell, "Frank, don't forget you promised us we could use the woman!" Stillwell replied, "Yes, yes, get at it, but hurry up! We got lots of work to do! We got to clean this mess up!" Stillwell gave each man a turn. Then he cut Abby's throat.

After burying both bodies in a common grave, miles away from the house, Stillwell reported back to Booker, "It's all done, boss. You won't be having any more problems with Canton or his old lady." Booker slid five $20 gold pieces across the desk. He grinned, "Here's a little something for you and the boys for a job well done!" Stillwell thought, "I ain't giving them sum bitches nothing. They already got their reward."

Booker was always interested in expanding his financial holdings. Some men are motivated by ambition. Booker was motivated by greed and selfishness. He couldn't stand to see someone prosper if it cost him a dollar.

The Stanley Hardware Store was thriving. It provided good value, but more importantly Spencer, his wife Tammy and their twin daughters Mia and Tia, became the town's favorite family. The sight of the steady stream of customers infuriated Booker. He muttered, "I helped start that store. It should have been mine!"

The bank funded a small loan to help Spencer build his store. Booker anticipated taking it over at the first sign of financial difficulty. That dream ended when Spencer set down a stack of cash on Booker's desk. Spencer exclaimed, "Good news, Mr. Booker! I'm here to pay off my note!" Booker faked a smile, "That's just great, Mr. Stanley. Congratulations!" Spencer added, "Tammy said to tell you how much we appreciate you getting us started." Booker replied, "Please tell Mrs. Stanley, thank you for the kind words."

Everyone one in town was shocked when Anita Owens opened up a competing hardware store across the street from Stanley's. Up until that time, Anita was the schoolmarm at the local school. Some people were asking, "How does a schoolteacher come up with the money to open that store?" Others wanted to know, "Where are we going to find another teacher?"

What folks in Marfa didn't realize was behind the sweet face of Anita Owens was a conniving cutthroat. Further, she was the secret lover of J.B. Booker. Booker kept a room reserved in the West Wind Hotel for their nightly rendezvous. Confidentiality was not a problem as the bank held a mortgage on the hotel. Booker told her, "I'm going to put you into the hardware business. I will be your silent partner no one knows about. Do as I say and you will be rich!" Anita answered with a deep kiss.

Later, Anita asked, "J.B., honey, the Stanley's are very popular. How am I going to be able to compete with them?" Booker smiled as he stroked her hair, "Don't you worry your pretty little head about that. Ol' J.B. will take care of that."

The first day Anita's Hardware opened up, Anita stood in the doorway of her store looking at no customers in her establishment. She compared that with the steady flow of people going in and out of Stanley's across the street. Anita impatiently tapped her foot, "Come on, J.B. I'm waiting on you. Where's my buyers?" That night Anita angrily declared to her lover, "I stayed in that damn store all day! Not one customer!" Booker smiled, "All in good time, my darling. All in good time. In the meantime you have other business to take care of...me!" In the wee hours of the morning, a commotion outside woke up Booker and Anita. Anita sleepily asked, "What's going on out there?" Booker grinned, "That's just the sound of drumming up your buyers." Anita went back to sleep. She thought whatever it was, could wait till the next day.

By the time anyone could respond to the fire, Stanley's Hardware Store was engulfed in flames. Nothing could be saved. It was a total loss. From the hotel window Anita could see people lined up to get in her store. She asked Booker, "I'm going to be swamped! How should I handle it?" Booker grinned, "Go up on your prices."

Spencer Stanley was already waiting on Booker when he arrived at the bank. Booker shook his hand, "I'm so sorry about what happened to your store. Come back to my office where we can talk." When they were seated, Booker looked sympathetic, "How can I help you, Mr. Stanley?" Spencer replied, "That's the reason I'm here. I need another loan to rebuild my store and get back into business." Booker mused for a minute. He sighed, "I was afraid of that. The economy in the state of Texas is not good at the present time. I regret that the bank is not in a position to grant you a loan."

Spencer was stunned, "But...but...I already had one loan with y'all. I paid it off before it was even due. I thought for sure the bank would loan me the money to start over!" Booker shook his head, "Sorry, I can't approve a loan right now. You might try back in six months." Spencer rose to his feet, "Six months? I can't wait six months! I have a wife and two children! We won't make it six days much less six months! Everything we had was tied up in the inventory of the store!" Booker shrugged, "That wasn't very prudent of you to leave all your assets in the inventory."

When the community heard about the plight of the Stanley family, several prominent men stepped forward with offers of loans to help rebuild the store. Within 48 hours each man who had made an offer was dead, shot down from ambush. Someone whispered, "Somehow that damn Booker and his sheriff are mixed up in this. They're a couple of snakes if I ever seen one."

Jake and Caleb Burk saw the strange wagon parked next to the corral when they rode in at dusk. There were a number of people sitting on the porch with Anne and Burk. When the boys walked up the steps, Anne motioned with her hand, "Jake, you remember my cousin Tammy, her husband Spencer and their two girls Mia and Tia?" Jake and Caleb Burk shook hands all around. Jake answered, "Sure I do. You folks came through about six months ago, headed out west to open a hardware store."

Burk blustered, "Yes and way they was treated is a durn shame! Somebody needs to be horsewhipped!" Jake furrowed his brow, "What happened?" Spencer replied, "We settled in Marfa, a good town with good folks. We opened up a store and it was a Going Jesse!..But we got burned out. As close as we can figure it was a greedy banker and his crooked sheriff. Several men offered to help us put the store back, but they were bushwhacked! We figured we couldn't beat a stacked deck so we left. Me and Tammy didn't want any more folks killed or hurt on our account."

Anne and Burk recognized the look in Jake's eyes. They didn't say anything, but they both knew what was coming. After supper Jake said, "Why don't you folks stay with us for a while. I'll ride out to Marfa. Maybe you can still make a go of it there. I'm pretty good at persuading people to listen to reason." Burk snorted, "That's the first time I ever heard it called 'persuading!'"

Tammy grasped Anne's hand, "Honey, we can't let y'all get involved. It's too dangerous." Anne responded with a laugh, "I know my husband. He's going to Marfa come hell or high water. Y'all just stay here with us. Jake won't be gone long." Spencer added, "Can I go and help, Jake?" Jake shook his head, "I appreciate it, but I need to go it alone." Burk grinned, "Yeah, the boy will be too busy 'persuading." Caleb Burk asked, "Pa?" Jake smiled, "Not yet but soon."

Jake hitched Buck to the rail under the sign that said "Sheriff's Office." Jake had considered how he wanted to handle this confrontation as he rode west. Usually, he preferred privacy. Instead he told Buck, "Since this bunch seems to have the town buffaloed, I need to do my cleanup in public. Next time those folks might stand up on their own. They need to learn to stomp their own snakes." Buck wasn't paying much attention. The only thing that did get Buck's attention is if Jake was late on doling out his bate of oats. Buck registered his displeasure by tossing his head accompanied by several disgusted whinnies.

Stillwell and two of his deputies jumped when they were started by the abrupt opening of the front door. The door banged against the back wall. Stillwell exclaimed,

"What the hell you think you're doing coming in my office like that? I should throw you in a cell!"

Jake's hand hovered over his Colt. He laughed, "I'd like to see you try it!" Stillwell retorted, "Who the hell are you?" Jake replied, "That's not your concern. You have a bigger problem than that. In one hour I want you out on the street. Your time running roughshod over the people of Marfa is done. One hour! Make sure your gun is loaded although you won't need all the bullets...By the way, bring these two Little Mary's with you. I reckon they probably need killing too!" Jake backed out the door, "One hour! Don't make me come get you!"

A passerby heard everything Jake said. He lit out to spread the word of the impending gunfight. Within 30 minutes, a mob had gathered in the street. Someone in the crowd said, "Maybe Stillwell will get what's been coming to him." After seeing Jake leaned up against the hitching post, stroking Buck's mane, another voice shouted, "Good Lord Almighty! That there is Jake Jackson! I seen him once in Ft. Worth!" A third voice stated, "That can't be Jake Jackson! I heared he was dead!"

Jake moved to the middle of the street. He carefully watched the windows of the sheriff's office. Jake figured drygulching would be something a skunk like Stillwell would do. People scurried to get out of the line of fire. Jake shouted, "Your time is up, Sheriff! Come out and face me!"

Stillwell ordered one of his deputies, "Slip out the back and see if you can get a shot from the alley. He wouldn't be the first you ever bushwhacked!" The deputy slowly opened the back door, but quickly slammed it shut. He

28

exclaimed, "Boss, there's a passel of hombres out there! I think they're mad!"

The Sheriff mopped the sweat off his face, "Okay, I don't care how fast this sum bitch is, he can't get us all if we stick together. Y'all follow me out the front door. One of you to the right of me. The other to the left. When I say, 'now', everybody draws and fires. One of us is bound to plug him!"

The milling crowd became motionless and silent when the front door of the sheriff's office creaked open. Sheriff Stillwell and his two deputies stepped out on the porch. He announced, "Mister, I'm placing you under arrest!...I also seen them that were all for this gunfight. When I get finished with him, I'll be dealing with you!" Stillwell muttered, "Now."

There were plenty of eyewitnesses that day. No one could remember seeing Jake actually pull his pistol. One man said later at a packed Yellow Dog, "It ain't often a man gets to see a gunfighter with Jackson's reputation. I was studying him hard. I ain't never saw his hand move. His Colt just appeared in his hand and began spitting bullets!"

Stillwell was fast. His gun almost cleared his holster when a .45 slug drilled into his right eye. The bullet exited from the back of his skull, raining blood on his two deputies. The other two didn't have much experience gunfighting. Their expertise was in back-shooting. Jake quickly fanned the hammer of his pistol, sending two bullets speeding towards his opponents. Each deputy had a round bullet hole perfectly placed between their eyes.

As all three of the hated lawmen crumpled on the porch in death, the crowd took in the smell of the gunfire and watched the gunsmoke drift skyward. Suddenly there was a raucous eruption of cheering and shouting. Some of the folks were literally dancing in the street with joy.

Booker had watched the scene unfold from a window in the bank. Anita saw everything as she stood in front of her hardware store. The crowd began to chant, "Booker! Booker! Booker!" They pounded each other on the back when Jake started towards the bank.

Booker commanded his head teller, "Don't let that man I'm here! Tell him I'm out for the day!" When Jake strode through the front door, the head teller slyly pointed towards Booker's office. Jake kicked in the door. Booker was cowering behind his desk. He begged, "Don't do nothing to me! None of this was my fault! It was all Stillwell's doings!" Jake retorted, "You are a liar. Today you answer for all the people you swindled." Booker screamed, "No, don't! I'll do anything! Whatever you want, I'll do it!"

Jake thought for a minute, "I want you to sign over the bank. Leave the buyer blank. The town will be the new owner. They can elect who they want to run the bank. I also want you to transfer ownership of the hardware to Spencer Stanley." Booker stuttered, "We..well...I don't know if I can legally do that." Jake cocked his Colt. Booker held up a hand, "Okay, okay...I'll do what you want."

When the paperwork was signed, Jake had asked for the crowd to select three men to witness the transaction. Afterwards Jake exclaimed to the ex-banker, "Get out of town! Take that Jezebel at the hardware store with you." Booker asked, "Am I going to be safe?" Jake responded, "No one's going to touch you as you're leaving. Now, get!"

As Booker and Anita warmed their hands around the campfire that night, Anita asked, "What are we gonna do now? We don't have a penny to our names!" Booker snorted, "Don't talk like a little fool! I have money in several banks. I'm going to hire an army of killers to kill Jake Jackson and get my town back! The folks in Marfa just think this is over. It's just started. Nobody gets the best of J.B. Booker!" Anita laughed, "I can't wait to see their faces when we take over Marfa again! I want to kill some of them myself!"

Jake stepped out of the darkness into the flickering firelight. He stated, "That's just about what I figured." Booker panicked, "Now hold on, Jackson! I did what you asked. You don't have any call to brace me!" Anita added as she arched her back, "If we need to sweeten the pot more, I can do that!"

Jake responded, "Booker, I took your property to repay for the property you stole. That doesn't count towards the people you had killed. That's going to take blood for blood. I learned that at an early age living with the Comanche. Women are held accountable too."

Jake snapped off two shots. The heads of Booker and Anita exploded from the force of the bullets. Both bodies fell into the campfire. The distinct odor of burning hair could be smelled.

Everyone was inside the big house except for Burk and Caleb Burk who were sitting on the porch. Caleb Burk popped up from his chair. He exclaimed excitedly, "It's Pa!...Ma, Pa's coming!" Anne and the Stanley family rushed out of the screen door onto the porch.

Jake tousled Caleb Burk's hair, "Howdy, son. It's sure good to see you. Take care of Buck for me." Caleb Burk grabbed Buck's reins, "Did you get em, Pa?" Jake smiled,

"I got em." Anne hugged Jake. As she kissed him, she whispered, "Welcome home, cowboy." Jake shook Burk's hand. Burk frowned, "The work has piled up around here with you gone." Jake laughed, "Good to see you too, Burk."

Spencer pumped Jake's hand, "I'm glad you made it back! I hope the trip wasn't too much trouble." Jake grinned, "No trouble atall. You'll be glad to know that your new hardware store is waiting on y'all back in Marfa. The Sheriff and his cronies have taken up residence in boot hill." Spencer was stunned, "What about Booker?" Jake replied, "J.B. Booker was the one who signed over the deed to your new store. He also signed over ownership of the bank to the citizens of Marfa."

Spencer embraced Tammy and the girls, "Thanks to Jake, it looks like we're going home!" Tammy tearfully gave Jake a hug. Spencer asked, "What happened to Booker?" Jake stated, "Rumor has it, he and his woman came to a bad end." When Spencer looked puzzled, Burk said, "When an Indian says rumored, he means…" Burk pulled his finger across his throat in a cutting motion.

Charlie Storms was a gambler by trade, but he fancied himself as a shootist of the highest order. Charlie built his reputation in Dodge City, Kansas. He killed for sport and for money. Some noted that face-to-face gunfights were carefully selected by Charlie for his opponent's lack of prowess with a gun. It was rumored that his hired killings were distinguished by bullet holes in the backs of the victims.

The young boy eagerly put his hands on the bar at the Long Branch Saloon. The kid had an old pistol stuck in a rope belt. He said, "Barkeep, I'm finally old enough to drink my first beer! Give me a tall one!" Fred the bartender, knew the boy. Fred asked, "Luke, does your Ma know you're in here?" Luke's ears turned red, "Fred, I'm a growed man now. My Ma don't have a say on where I go and what I do!" Fred shrugged, poured the beer and slid it down the bar to Luke. Luke tried not to make a bitter face as he downed his beer. He wiped his mouth with the back of his sleeve, "Gimme another one, Fred!"

When Fred refused to sell Luke his fourth beer, Luke retorted, "Dammit, Fred, I done told you I was a man. Growed men drink as many beers as they want!" Charlie grinned, "Hey kid, come over here. I need to teach you how to play poker. Every real man knows how to play." Luke bowed up, "Who you calling a kid, mister? I ain't no kid!"

Luke didn't know it, but he was being led by Charlie. Charlie replied, "Sure, son, sure. No offense intended." Luke responded angrily, "I ain't your son neither! I ain't got no Pa. He runned off when I was a button. I don't need no Pa. If I did, he wouldn't be the likes of you!" Charlie tried to conceal his smile, "Kid, them's fighting words. You any good at backing up your big mouth?"

Fred intervened, "Charlie, don't pay him no nevermind. He's just a kid." Three beers to someone who never drank a beer before, caused Luke to lose all the checks and balances in his judgement. Luke exploded, "I ain't no kid!...and mister, I'll fight you right now!" Luke balled up his fists. Charlie shook his head as he laughed, "Fighting with your fists is what a kid does. Real men use guns...What about it, kid? You know how to use that hogleg you're wearing?"

Luke paused as he thought about how that old pistol pulled a little to the left when fired. Charlie grinned,

"That's what I thought. You talk big, but you're just a kid who's still wet behind the ears!" Charlie let the boy draw his gun and cock it. Charlie thought, "Can't nobody say he didn't have a chance." Charlie jerked and triggered his sixgun. The first bullet centered the boy's belly. Luke squealed in pain, "I'm shot! I'm shot!"

Luke staggered before falling on his back. He clutched the hole in his stomach as he moaned, "It hurts!" Charlie stood over him and smiled, "Yep, getting shot in the belly stings like a sum bitch!" Fred shouted, "Somebody go get Doc!" Charlie scowled, "Ain't gonna do no good. The kid's a goner!" Luke futilely tried to stop the bleeding with his hands. He began to cry, "I don't want to die...I don't want to die." Luke looked just like what he was, a little boy who wanted his Ma.

Charlie told Marshal Tanner, "Marshal, it was self-defense. The man had his gun out getting ready to shoot me. I had no choice. It was him or me!" Marshal Tanner turned to the bartender, "Fred?" Fred reluctantly nodded his head, "I reckon it was like Charlie said. Luke had cocked his pistol."

The Marshal stared at Charlie before he spoke, "Storms, I done had my fill of you. First, this weren't no man. This was just a boy. Second, any fool could see this boy wasn't a gun hand. You murdered this kid who was too damn dumb to know to walk away. I want you out of Dodge by noon tomorrow. I don't care where you go just as long as you become somebody else's problem!"

Later that night, Marshal Tanner heard a whisper from a dark alley, "Hey, marshal." Tanner squinted as he tried to see, "What do you want? Come out here where I can get a look at you." The gun blast shattered the stillness of the night. The bullet passed through his marshal's badge and penetrated his heart. The Marshal coughed a few times as he spit up blood. He crumpled to the dirt, dead on his feet." The voice chuckled, "Hard to be giving orders from the grave, ain't it?"

The next day Charlie pushed through the batwing doors at the Long Branch and took his seat at his customary table. Fred looked up in surprise from polishing glasses. He asked, "I thought the Marshal posted you out of town?" Charlie grinned, "The way I hear it, Marshal Tanner ain't in no position to do anything about it." Fred frowned, "I guess you heard about the Marshal getting bushwhacked last night." Charlie continued to smile, "Yep...Some people just don't have no respect for the law."

Burl Fuller didn't come in the Long Branch much. He preferred to do his drinking at his mansion on the edge of town or at private parties with his well-heeled friends. He approached the bar and asked, "Bartender, I'm looking for a man who goes by the name of Charlie Storms. I heard he frequents your establishment. Do you know him or where I can find him?" Fred grimaced as he tilted his head toward Charlie's table.

Meeting with a notorious gunman was a new experience for Burl. He started to lose the confidence that comes from being wealthy as he approached Charlie. Burl froze in front of Charlie's table. Charlie noted the expensive clothes. His eyes narrowed, "Something I can do for you?" Burl stammered, "Uh..are..are you Charlie Storms?" Charlie replied, "Who wants to know?" Burl stuck out his hand, "I'm Burl Fuller." Burl expected Charlie to know who he was. Instead Charlie ignored his hand, "So?"

Burl awkwardly withdrew his hand. He cleared his throat, "I have a proposition for you, Mr. Storms. It would mean some money in your pocket." Charlie kicked out a chair from his table towards Burl. He smiled, "Have a seat, Mr. Fuller."

After sitting down, Burl leaned in and said in hushed tones, "Mr. Storms, I'm a man of many financial holdings. I've heard that you have special skills that I may need. I own a coal mine in north Texas, Bridgeport to be exact. I received a notice of a lawsuit from an attorney in Ft. Worth. He represents a man who claims to have a mineral deed that would give him ownership of my mine. My concern is he may be right. I don't want to lose that coal mine, Mr. Storms. It's a good money maker. I will pay you $10,000 to get it all…sorted out."

Charlie gave a low whistle, "$10,000? I believe I can get things sorted out to suit you for that kind of money." Burl remarked, "Good…I will give you $5,000 now. You'll get the other $5,000 when the job is finished. When can you leave?" Charlie grinned, "As soon as I get my money."

William and Linda Young sat in the law office of Sanford Collins in downtown Ft. Worth. William said, "Mr. Collins, I hope you don't mind us dropping in on you like this. We were wondering how the lawsuit for the coal mine was going." Sanford replied, "You were lucky to catch me between court cases. We served the registered owner, Mr. Burl Fuller of Dodge City, Kansas. So far he hasn't responded, but he's got 30 days to do so. I do think you stand an excellent chance to take possession of the mine. If we prevail in court, you also may be eligible to collect damages for what the mine has produced in the past."

William and Linda exchanged glances. Linda stated, "I don't know, Mr. Collins. That doesn't seem fair that we should collect back money too." Collins responded, "On the contrary, Mrs. Young. In my opinion the mineral deed Fuller was operating under was fraudulent. Crooks don't get to keep what they stole in the past."

William and Linda held hands on the buggy ride back to their small farm, north of Ft. Worth. Upon the death of Linda's father, Harold, she inherited the 200 acres and house. It was when she was cleaning out the closets after her father's passing that Linda found the mineral deed.

William had heard that Sanford Collins was an outstanding attorney. After Collins examined the deed, .he checked it against the legal description of the coal mine in Bridgeport. Even the buttoned-up lawyer couldn't suppress a smile at the prospects of capturing the mine.

When Charlie arrived in Ft. Worth, the first thing he did was tie his horse up in front of the White Elephant Saloon. Charlie had ran out of whiskey two days ago. His body demanded rot-gut. After gulping down the first couple of shots, Charlie slowed down enough to sip the next one. The bartender had commented, "Been a while?"

Charlie's ears perked up when he heard the bartender say to one of the cowboys, "Yep, most folks have heard about the people claiming to own the big coal mine up in Bridgeport. Wouldn't that be something to wake up one morning and suddenly be rich? If that happened to me, I durn sure wouldn't be slinging drinks to the likes of you!" The cowboy laughed, "You and me both, pard!"

Later Charlie cautiously asked the barkeep, "Say, I believe I heared about them folks claiming that mine. Their name was...Rung or Young...something like that."

The bartender replied, "It was Young. William and Linda Young. They've become famous in these parts. As soon as old Sanford Collins filed that lawsuit, word spread like wildfire. Old Sanford is the best lawyer in Texas. When folks found out he was involved, they figured going to court would be a done deal."

Charlie smiled, "Sounds like they was mighty lucky...By the way, where are the Young's from?" The bartender replied, "Oh, they're from here. They got a small farm a few miles north of here up Sandy Creek." Charlie nodded. The bartender laughed, "If you're thinking about paying them a visit to get a loan or something, let me save you the trip. They've had so many people visit them trying to get a piece of that mine, they've locked their gate and hung up a "no trespassing" sign." Charlie raised an eyebrow, "Can't say that I blame them."

Their dog, Old Cur began to bark furiously. Linda exclaimed, "Land sakes alive! What is Old Cur barking at now? I swear sometimes that dog barks just to hear himself bark!" Since he could see the gate from the front window of the house, William pulled back the drape. He remarked, "I don't see anything. The gate's still closed. Old Cur might have seen a jackrabbit...Anyways, nothing for us to be alarmed about. He'll shut up after a while."

Old Cur piled off the porch and rushed to the side of the house. Charlie was waiting there with a hoe that had been leaning against a fence. The first swing caught Old Cur high in the neck, right behind his head. After a small yelp, the second blow silenced the dog for good.

In the house William responded to the quiet, "See there. I told you it was nothing. That danged dog finally shut up. He was starting to get on my nerves." Linda replied, "William, go check on him. I thought I heard him yelp." William was aggravated, "Sure thing. Anything else I can do for you while I'm up? Bake you a cake?" Linda giggled as William stepped out on the porch, "Old Cur, dammit, come here!"

When he didn't get a response, William muttered, "Damn dog." He looked around the side of house. As his eyes adjusted to the darkness, William saw a dark form on the ground. He asked, "Old Cur, is that you?" William knelt down and turned over the bloodied body of Old Cur. A voice stated, "You're the reason your dog is dead. You should of minded your own business." That was the last thing William heard. The bullet from Charlie's pistol put out the light in William's eyes.

At the retort of the gun blast, a panicked Linda screamed, "William!" Charlie was waiting for her around the corner of the house. He grabbed her wrist, "You needn't worry none about them two. They're both dead. You folks would have been a lot better off by just tending to your own knitting!" Charlie knocked her unconscious with the barrel of his gun. He dragged Linda back inside where he violated her. When he was finished, Charlie pumped two slugs into her chest.

Jake never had much use for lawyers. He didn't see the need for them. The Comanche didn't have any reason to doubt a man's word. If he said it, that was good enough for them. Burk insisted, "I want a will to make no mistake that you, Anne and Caleb Burk are to inherit the Four-Sixes when I die." Jake replied, "Well, why isn't one of the lawyers in Wichita Falls good enough to write the will. Why are you wanting me to go all the way to Ft. Worth to a lawyer there?" Burk blustered, "Cause I want Sanford Collins to do it! Everybody know he's the best, dang lawyer in Texas! Don't you want to see Caleb Burk is taken care of proper?" Jake threw up his hands, "Alright, alright! I'll go in the morning!" Jake muttered under his breath as he walked away, "He don't need no taking care of. The boy needs to learn to stomp his own snakes."

Jake was sitting in Sanford's office going over the details of the will when there was a loud knock at the door. Without waiting to be invited Sanford's secretary burst in, "Mr. Collins, it's just awful! William and Linda Young have been found murdered at their farm!" Sanford bolted upright out of his chair, "What?...How?...When?..." The secretary responded, "I don't know any of the details. The sheriff just brought in their bodies!"

Stunned, Sanford slumped back in his chair. Jake asked, "Would it be better if I came back another time?" Sanford raised a finger, "Please give me a minute." Sanford gave Jake a brief rundown of the circumstances regarding the Youngs, the coal mine and Burl Fuller. Sanford continued, "Mr. Jackson, I am aware of your talents. I would like to retain you." Jake shook his head, "Sorry, Mr. Collins, my gun is not for hire."

Sanford studied Jake's face. He responded, "Remarkable!...Mr. Jackson, I fear that myself and my family are in grave danger. I think William and Linda Young were killed by an agent for Mr. Fuller. Fuller is too wealthy to do something like that himself...As the attorney of record, I believe Fuller will try to have me killed too. I appreciate your stance on being compensated for your abilities. Would you consider helping me and my family out of a sense of justice?"

Jake didn't respond for a full five minutes. Finally he replied, "Mr. Collins, I can't make any guarantees, but I will look into it." Jake turned around as he started to leave, "Please send a wire to Anne Jackson and Burk Burnett to Wichita Falls. Tell them I'm fine, but that I may be gone longer than I anticipated. Tell them I'm helping a friend." Sanford replied, "I'll get that wire sent immediately...And, Mr. Jackson, thank you so much. I won't forget what you're doing for me."

Charlie considered killing Collins too, but decided that should be worth more than what Fuller was paying him. Charlie thought, "If killing them two was worth $10,000, I'm going back to Dodge to collect more money. Shooting the lawyer should be worth another $10,000." Charlie rode hard until he got well into Oklahoma. After several days of checking his backtrail, Charlie began to relax.

The tracks leading away from the Young's farm were easy to follow. Jake told Buck, "Any Comanche boy could follow this trail." Buck liked to travel cross country. It gave him a chance to stretch his legs. Buck favored it over roping cattle. The horse had been known to bite a cow if given an opportunity.

After stuffing himself with bacon and pan fried bread, Charlie fell into a deep sleep by the warm campfire. He dreamed about money, fancy hotels and fancy women. One of the women started poking him in the neck with something sharp. Charlie mumbled, "Stop that. That don't feel good."

Charlie became completely awake when the voice of Jake Jackson exclaimed, "It ain't supposed to feel good, jasper!" Charlie realized the pain in his neck was being caused by the blade of Jake's skinning knife. Charlie swallowed hard. He asked, "Who are you, mister? What do you want?" Jake replied, "I want to know who paid you to kill those poor folks at that farm in Ft. Worth?" Charlie snorted, "I got no idee what you're talking about!"

Jake increased the pressure of the knife on the tender skin of Charlie's throat. Jake continued, "I think you do. You can do yourself a favor by telling me now." Charlie tried to spit, "I ain't telling you nothing, sum bitch!" The blade began to cut into Charlie's neck. As the blood started to flow, Jake added, "You're gonna tell me what I want to know. If cutting your throat doesn't work, I'll begin slicing off body parts that you probably favor."

Jake turned the knife around and struck Charlie on the head with the butt of his skinner. When Charlie regained consciousness, he was tied out spread-eagled and naked. Charlie stuttered, "Wh...what are you going to do?" Jake flicked Charlie's private parts with the sharp edge of his knife. Jake replied, "What do you think I'm going to do? Whatever you think it is, it's going to be much worse than that. I was raised Comanche. We have our ways."

Charlie offered, "I got money. Lots of it. If it ain't enough, I can get more!" Jake shook his head, "I got money. All I'll ever need. There ain't gonna be no deals. You tell me what I want or you'll end up just a body with a head on top. Nothing else. I know how to make this last for at least a week. It's up to you."

Charlie started to sob, "Okay, you win. Just don't hurt me. Mr. Burl Fuller of Dodge City, Kansas, paid me to kill them farmers. He said he owned some kind of big mine and the Youngs was trying to take it...Now, I told you what you wanted. Turn me loose!" Jake smiled, "I promised a friend, justice. Letting you go wouldn't exactly be justice, would it? The good news is I'm only going to cut off one thing."

Jake hung Charlie's head by the hair from a nearby tree as a warning to others not to take advantage of those who couldn't protect themselves. The head dripped blood for almost an hour. The headless body was still staked out, but twitched like frog legs on a hot skillet.

Jake stood in front of the impressive, stone office building in Dodge City. The overhead sign said "Fuller Enterprises." Jake entered the wood-paneled foyer. The attractive receptionist looked down her nose at the rugged cowboy. She sniffed, "May I help you, sir?"

Jake didn't answer. He strode past her desk and threw open one of the double office doors. The receptionist jumped up from her chair. She protested as she followed Jake in the office, "Sir, this will not do! You can't see Mr. Fuller without an appointment!" The startled Fuller's eyes widened as he searched the intruder's face. The receptionist declared, "I'm so sorry, Mr. Fuller! Do you want me to summon Sheriff Hopkins?" Jake spoke, "This is about the coal mine in Texas."

The color drained from Fuller's countenance. He stated, "No, Miss Powell. That will be all for now." Fuller addressed Jake, "Alright, Mister...Mister...whatever your name is. What's this about my mine?" Jake made himself at home on the overstuffed, leather couch. Jake smiled, "The truth is that's not really your mine, is it?" Fuller blustered, "That's preposterous! Of course it's my mine! I have a legal deed to it."

Jake stood up as he became more serious, "There's a lawyer in Texas who says otherwise. Sanford Collins says that your deed is a fraud and that he holds the real deed to the mine." Fuller retorted, "I have a whole team of lawyers that will substantiate my deed in court!" Jake responded, "Too thin, Fuller. I have a confession from

Charlie Storms. He said you paid him $10,000 to murder William and Linda Young."

Fuller studied his folded hands, "And where is this Storms fellow?" Jake replied, "After I removed his head, I tied it to a live-oak tree in Oklahoma." Fuller fearfully asked, "Why would you do something as horrible as that?" Jake replied, "I was raised Comanche. There are worst things I could have done to him. The Great Spirit teaches us that what a man does in life comes back to him."

Something clicked in Fuller's brain, "Wait a minute! I know who you are now! You're Jake Jackson! I've heard about you, but I thought you were dead." Jake responded, "That's enough talk. Get up. You're going back to Texas for trial." Fuller became desperate, "Wait a minute, Mr. Jackson! I am a wealthy man. I can make you rich. How much money do you want?" Jake replied, "I have money. Get up!"

Fuller opened the middle drawer of his desk, "I don't think you understand how much money I'm talking about!...Let me get a check..." Fuller grabbed the pearl-handled Derringer. As he started to point it at Jake, a .45 slug blew off the top of his head.

The panicked receptionist rushed into the room. She screamed as she saw parts of her employer's skull scattered around the expensive carpet. Jake held up a finger, "Now you can go get the Sheriff." After Jake explained the complete story to Sheriff Wiggins, Wiggins gave a low whistle, "Man, that's quite a tale! I appreciate you wanting me to wire that attorney. That won't be necessary. If you weren't telling me the truth, I don't reckon you'd of stuck around. Besides, it ain't every day that a feller can tell his grandkids that he met Jake Jackson!"

Yuma, Litsu and Goshe were three young Apache braves who chafed under the restrictions of the Indian reservation at Ft. Sill, Oklahoma. They were the last of the free Apaches confined to the reservation when their leader, Geronimo was incarcerated at the Fort.

Yuma declared, "I cannot take this kind of life. There are no mountains or prairies to roam. The soldiers have even taken my pony! We are fed scraps like dogs. I would rather be dead!" Litsu responded, "This is no life for an Apache! We have got to find a way to escape." Goshe frowned, "We will need to be careful. We don't want to be locked away in a little room like Geronimo. He was once a great, war chief. Now the white eyes have shamed him."

Sgt. Greeley growled, "Ain't I told you three to stop all that sneaking around? There's no call for y'all to be meeting like you got something important to say. Now get back to your own teepees before I take the butt of my rifle to you!" Greeley muttered as the Apache left, "If I had my way, I'd hang the lot of you. Bunch of damn savages. Ain't good for nothing."

In a couple of days, the three Apache were able to huddle again. Yuma whispered, "We leave tonight. I have gathered a few knives and one bow with arrows. That will help us start. Later we can make more. Say nothing to no one, not even the old ones. I will scratch at your teepee." Litsu asked, "What about ponies? Won't we need to steal horses to get away?" Yuma shook his head, "No, a horse would be too easy to track. Some of the traitors in our own people might help the soldiers find us. We walk. We become one with the earth. We kill anyone who follows us. Tonight we go back to being true Apache."

That night wasn't picked at random. It was moonless and cloudy. The clouds blotted out the starlight. Litsu and Goshe silently slipped from their teepees at the signal. Yuma motioned them to stay and wait for him.

After carefully checking to see that no one was watching, Sgt. Greeley quickly tipped up the flask and gulped the whiskey. He thought, "I hate guard duty, especially guarding these dirty Indians." Greeley was dozing at his post when he felt a sharp sting on his neck. He lifted his hand to his throat to see what caused the pain. When he pulled it down, his hand was drenched in blood. As consciousness started to drift away in the inky night, Greeley never realized his throat had been cut.

The Apache stayed in a dog trot all night, before stopping to rest right before dawn. Even though it was at night and the night was dark, the braves were careful where they stepped. Yuma arranged three stones that only another Apache would notice. The stones warned that death was waiting on any that followed them. Yuma whispered, "If any traitor from our tribe is tracking us to help the horse soldiers, this is a sign we are protected by the Great Spirit."

The next morning Capt. Leonard Cox spoke to the assembled Apache, "Last night one of our brave soldiers was murdered in cold blood. Because they are absent, we know it was Yuma, Litsu and Goshe. I need a tracker. It will mean double rations for a month for the man and his family." Most of the tribe stared straight ahead. A few looked at the Captain. Ilesh spoke, "I will go." Ilesh hated Yuma. He was jealous that Yuma was held in high esteem by the tribe and Ilesh was not.

Capt. Cox called Lt. Dickerson and Sgt. Carter into his office. Cox angrily commanded, "I want you men to take Second Platoon and catch these renegades. When you find them, shoot them or hang them. Just don't bring them back here! That damn Yuma is always trying to stir something up...And when Ilesh is no longer useful, kill him too. I hate a back-stabber!"

Second Platoon answered the call to arms. They left the reservation with their Apache scout out front. At first things went well until Ilesh saw the warning stones left by Yuma. He milled around for a couple of hours before turning to Lt. Dickerson, "The trail has gone cold. I have lost it."

Lt. Dickerson scowled, "Well, I guess we have no further use for you...Sgt. Carter." Sgt. Carter unsnapped the flap on his holster, pulled the Walker Colt and shot a surprised Ilesh in the face. Lt. Dickerson announced to the troopers, "I will be filing a report when we get back to Ft. Sill that our Apache scout deserted us and his whereabouts is unknown." As they rode off, one trooper whispered, "There's one good Indian." Another trooper couldn't suppress a small laugh.

The next few days there were no conversations among the braves. They communicated by sign language or sometimes a simple look would speak intentions. Litsu killed a jackrabbit with the bow and a well-placed arrow. Instead of risking a fire, they ate the meat and entrails raw.

From a far ridge, the Apache watched the ranch come to life and began a new day. A dozen cowboys saddled horses and rode off. Yuma spoke in a soft voice, "There is only the old man, the woman and the boy still there. We will kill the old man and capture the woman as a squaw. If the boy proves worthy, he can be an Apache warrior. If he is not fit, we will kill him too."

Goshe nodded, "Your plan is good. We are warriors. It is time to take scalps and captives." The braves began to creep their way to the barn. The boy was feeding horses. Yuma knocked him unconscious with a rock. Litsu flipped him on his belly. He used a few rawhide strings hanging from a stall door to tie the boy's hands behind his back.

Burk was napping in his rocker after a big breakfast when an arrow thudded into his thigh. The peaceful morning was shattered by Apache war whoops. Anne ran out the front door, tossing a lever-action rifle to Burk. She began cocking and firing a pistol at the three Apache who were hunkered down behind saddles hanging from the bottom rail of the corral. Burk levered his rifle as fast as he could. The air was filled with the angry buzzing of bullets.

Anne screamed, "Caleb Burk! Caleb Burk! Where are you?" Yuma muttered to the other two braves, "Come. We cannot fight these guns without guns of our own. We will take horses and the boy."

Anne watched in horror as the Indians rode off with Caleb Burk tied over a horse. She grabbed Burk's arm, "Pa, they got Caleb Burk!" Burk got up, "Let me get my horse!" Burk collapsed with the arrow still in his leg. Anne's eyes narrowed as she watched the raiders ride out of sight with their hostage.

Burk struggled to get up. Anne restrained him with a hand on his shoulder. She exclaimed, "Pa, you're in no condition to go after them! I'll tend to your wound...Jake should be back any day now. He will get my boy back."

A group of the ranch hands galloped up. Shorty asked, "What's all the shooting about?" Anne was working on Burk's leg. She replied, "Indians! They shot Burk and kidnapped Caleb Burk!" Shorty shouted, "C'mon boys! Let's go get the boy back!" Burk held up a hand. He yelled, "Hold on, durn it! All you're going to do is get my grandson killed. I'd shoot any man that done that! If them Indians know someone is after them, the first thing they'll do is kill Caleb Burk. We're gonna wait on Jake!"

Jake got back to the ranch that afternoon. He kept waiting to hear Caleb Burk announce that his Pa was back. His puzzled look turned to concern when he saw the bandage on Burk's leg and Anne's tear-stained face. Jake bailed off Buck. When he ran up the steps, Anne met him and wrapped her arms around her husband. Anne was desperate, "Oh, Jake! It was Indians! They shot Burke and carried away Caleb Burk!"

Jake turned to Burk, "Describe them to me." Burk retorted, "I don't need to describe them! I know Apache when I see em!" Jake asked, "How bad are you hurt?" Burk responded, "I'm fine! Quit farting around with me! Go get my grandson!"

Jake looked over the rest of the horses in the corral. Even though they had just come off a long trip, Jake elected to ride Buck. He pulled off the saddle and fed Buck a ration of oats. Anne was pacing back and forth, "Honey, please hurry." Jake responded, "I need the best horse under me. Buck is the best horse, but he needs to eat first.

Jake went in the house. When he came out, he wore only a loin cloth. Burk breathed a sigh of relief when he saw Jake in Comanche war paint. Normally it made Anne nervous when Jake went Comanche. This time it was comforting.

Yuma finally pulled back on the reins when his horse began to stumble due to exhaustion. He said, "We will rest our horses." After dismounting Yuma eyed his captive. Yuma spoke to the others, "We need to find out if we should kill this white boy or if we should let him live."

Yuma threatened his captive by waving a knife next to his eyes, "Will you cry like a woman if my knife bites you?" The other two Apache smirked. Yuma didn't know that Caleb Burk could understand him. Jake had taught him Comanche. The Apache language and the Comanche language were similar.

The look on Caleb Burk's face was stoic. He didn't flinch when Yuma dragged the point of the knife down the side of Caleb Burk's face making the blood run. The look on his face never changed. He was his father's son. After several more cuts with no reaction from Caleb Burk, Yuma stated, "This white boy will make a good Apache." That didn't stop Yuma from beating Caleb Burk with a large stick.

The Apache continually watched their backtrail for any tell-tale cloud of dust that could be an approaching band of men. Yuma checked his surroundings, "We will sleep here for a short time."

The hair on the back of Jake's neck stood up. He had always been able to sense a dangerous situation. At the same time Buck's ears suddenly pricked forward. Jake whispered to the horse, "Stay here." Jake slid off his back and dropped the reins. Jake resumed tracking on foot.

The Apache had built a small fire no larger than a hand. Its smell helped Jake pinpoint their location. The three Apache were huddled around the flame for warmth. Caleb Burk was tied to a nearby tree. Even in the dark, Jake could see his bloodied and bruised face. Jake was encouraged to see the rise and fall of his son's chest.

Jake flashed into the camp, slashing with his knife. Deep gashes gaped open on the throats of Litsu and Goshe. One minute they were breathing normally. The next they were gurgling blood. Jake pinned Yuma to the ground with the point of his knife pressed against his neck. Yuma croaked, "What are you? Are you a demon spirit?" Jake smiled, "I am known as White Wolf." Jake saw the recognition in Yuma's eyes before plunging his blade so far into the Apache's neck that it severed his spine.

As Yuma kicked his last, Jake looked up at Caleb Burk, "Are you alright, son?" Caleb Burk grinned, "Be glad it's not Grandpa! Cause he would say, 'It's about time!" Jake laughed out loud. He began to cut the bindings on his son, "Let's get you cleaned up a bit. Ma kept telling me to hurry up. I don't want her to think I didn't." This time Caleb Burk laughed out loud.

Caleb Burk proudly watched Jake take the scalps of the Apache. Jake tied them in Buck's mane.

Anne's heart skipped a beat when she saw two riders on the horizon. She had been watching faithfully for the return of her husband and son. Anne shrieked, "Pa, it's them! Pa, they're coming!" Anne went from one to the other frantically kissing each. Burk squeezed his grandson for a long time. He told Jake, "What took you so long?" Burk was puzzled at how hard Caleb Burk laughed at that.

Anne didn't say anything about the scalps until the next day. She quietly asked, "Did you have to scalp them?" Jake shrugged, "How else is the boy going to learn?"

Gunslinging came easy to David Watts. His Pa taught him the basics before Earl went back to prison for the last time. Earl threw around compliments like they were bank safes so Slick was surprised when his Pa praised him, "That's some pretty good shooting. Your draw is pretty slick too." Earl called his boy, Slick from then on. The nickname stuck.

Earl was a disagreeable sort. His last disagreement came to a head in prison when an inmate stuck a homemade knife in Earl's ribs. Slick's mother, Ester had died the previous year from consumption. When Slick got the news of his father's death, he was on his own at 16 years of age.

Buster Mathis held court every day in the Buckhorn Saloon in San Antonio, Texas. It was common knowledge that Buster was the leader of an outlaw gang that was famous for its ruthlessness. Slick pushed through the batwing doors. It wasn't hard to determine who Buster was. He was the one doing all the talking.

Slick walked up to his table and stood motionless. His shadow darkened Buster's table. That irritated Buster, "Kid, move or I'll move you!" Slick replied, "I'd like to see you try." At first there was stunned silence. Then someone giggled. That was followed by more and more laughing until everyone in the saloon was guffawing. Even Buster was slapping his knee in glee.

Finally Buster wiped the tears from his face, "Alright, kid. You gave us a good laugh. Now you need to skedaddle!" Slick still didn't move. Buster became exasperated, "Okay, kid, now you're starting to get on my nerves...What do you want?" Slick shrugged, "I figured since I was the fastest gun in Texas, you would want to hire me."

Buster raised an eyebrow, "You think you're faster than my man, Bart?...What do you say, Bart? Do you think this boy is faster than you?" Bart grinned, "Just say the word, Mr. Mathis. I'll put this whelp in his place." Buster smugly said, "How about it, kid? You want to pull on Bart?" Slick squared up on Bart, "It's his funeral."

The attitude in the saloon flip-flopped. Jovial and cheerful were replaced by anxious and concern as people scrambled to get out of the line of fire.

Bart frowned as he went for his gun. The pistol never cleared leather before a bullet slammed into Bart's mouth, splattering teeth and blood over those who didn't move far enough away. Just for good measure, Slick fanned the hammer twice more. One slug blasted off Bart's right ear, the other slug his left one. To complete the show, Slick rapidly twirled his sixshooter on one finger before gently dropping it back in his holster. A flabbergasted Buster finally gasped, "The hell you say!"

Buster studied Slick, "How do I know that wasn't just a one-time piece of luck? Do you think you can do that again?" Slick shrugged, "You got any more men you can afford to sacrifice?" Buster looked at his boys to see if there were any takers. Every man shook his head, no.

Buster mused, "Hmmm...One gunfight and you've got everybody scared shitless. Kid, what's your name?" Slick replied, "It's Watts...Slick Watts. My old man died in prison without a penny to his name. That ain't gonna happen to me!" Buster stuck out his hand, "Good to meet you, Slick. I can use a man like you. As of now, you are on my payroll." The outlaw gang leader looked at the remains of one of his gang members. He motioned to some of his men, "Drag this no-account out of here. I don't want to see him or smell him!"

The next day Buster told Slick, "There's a banker here in town that's gotten too big for his britches. He thinks he's too good to make me a loan. Hell, it ain't even his money. It's the bank's! A man in my position can't have nobody disrespecting him like that! I need to make an example out of him…Think you can get rid of him without getting your neck stretched?" Slick nodded, "There won't be no problem."

Andrew Mellon had opened the second bank in San Antonio. Unlike some bankers, Andrew was warm and friendly to everyone. Because he was so welcoming as well as being a hard worker, Andrew's bank prospered. That morning over breakfast, Andrew beamed at his wife, Kathy and his 15-year-old daughter, Lily, "I reckon I'm the luckiest fellow alive! Two beauties to come home to!" Kathy smiled at the husband who she loved with all her heart. Lily blushed, "Aww, Pa!"

When Andrew was helping an elderly woman understand how the bank protected her money, he was startled at the rudeness of the stranger. Slick declared, "I got a bone to pick with you, Mellon!" Andrew replied, "Just a minute, sir. I'll be right with you when I'm finished with this lady." Slick responded, "You are finished with her. You're just too damn dumb to know it!" Andrew addressed the woman, "Excuse me, ma'am. I'll be with you as soon as I can."

Andrew straightened his coat, "How can I help you, sir?" Slick grinned, "You can help me by not being such a low-down, yellow-bellied polecat!" Andrew reddened in embarrassment and anger, "Sir, I have no idea what you're talking about. I would thank you to change your tone when you speak to me!" Slick snorted, "I'll speak with you any damn way I please! If you don't like it, maybe you should do something about it. You ain't even carrying a gun. What kind of self-respecting man don't carry a gun? Are you a coward?" Andrew responded, "Sir, whatever the problem is, violence is not the answer."

Slick moved closer to Andrew and whispered so no one else could hear him, "When I'm done here, I'm gonna go to your house and help myself to your women. I'm especially looking forward to that young daughter of yours...Lily, ain't it? I'll probably be her first, but don't worry. I'll break her in right... A gun is the only way you can stop me."

An enraged Andrew ran into his office, retrieved a pistol that he kept in his desk and returned pointing the gun at Slick. Slick's hand was a blur as he drew and fired. The bullet liquefied Andrew's heart. Slick holstered his weapon. He smiled at the terrified tellers, "Somebody go fetch the Sheriff. This man just tried to kill me."

After Slick told his story to Sheriff Martin. The Sheriff asked the bank tellers their version. Though her tears, one of the tellers stated, "I don't know what got into Mr. Mellon. The man was rude, but I've seen Mr. Mellon handle rude customers before. I think it was something that the man whispered to Mr. Mellon. I couldn't hear what was said. Whatever was said seemed to make Mr. Mellon go mad. He did point a gun at the man...It was all just so horrible!"

Slick sauntered into the Buckhorn later that day. He casually took a seat at Buster's table. Slick smiled. "I took care of your problem." Buster laughed, "So I heard! Good job, Slick." Buster slid an envelope across the table, "Here's your money. If you keep up the good work, they'll be a lot more coming!" Slick opened the envelope. When he saw the $200, Slick nodded at Buster, "Whatever you need, boss."

Sheriff Jud Martin had just recently been elected sheriff. The previous sheriff had been killed under mysterious circumstances. He was found dead sitting at his office desk one morning. Someone had shot him in the back of the head, execution style.

Very little was known about Jud Martin's background. For some reason his candidacy was supported by some of the most influential men and families in San Antonio. It was a head-scratcher to most. Slick raised an eyebrow when he saw the exact same type of envelope that Buster gave Slick, sticking out of Sheriff Martin's vest pocket. That told Slick that he and the Sheriff were on the same side.

Carlos Lopez exclaimed, "I'm sick of hearing about Buster Mathis and his gringo gang!" Pablo shrugged, "I understand how you feel, but what can we do? He has more men...and he's white...And that's not the worst part. I heard Sheriff Martin in on Buster's payroll." Carlos snorted, "That doesn't give him and his pendejos the right to come into our side of town! We don't operate in white San Antonio. He's not supposed to poach in Mexican San Antonio!"

The Lopez gang hung out in Rosita's Cantina. Some Mexican woman are the shy, retiring type. Rosita was loud and boisterous, always quick with a wink and an off-color joke. She was well endowed and favored low cut blouses that displayed her assets. Despite her flirtatious ways, it was common knowledge that Rosita was Carlos's woman. Carlos had used his gun on more than one occasion on someone who didn't recognize the outlaw leader's property.

Carlos downed another shot of mescal. He addressed his men, "The gringos are taking from us what should be ours! Because they are white, they think they can rob and kill Mexicans on our side of town! They must be taught a lesson! Anytime you see a member of the gringo gang where they're not supposed to be, kill them!" Pablo replied, "But patron, won't that put us in a war with Buster Mathis and Sheriff Martin?" Carlos jerked his pistol from his belt and shot Pablo at point blank range. Carlos asked his stunned gang members, "Is there anyone else that wants to challenge my orders?" When everyone looked down or away, Carlos commanded, "Haul this hijo-de-puta out of my sight!"

Jack and Leon, members of the Mathis gang, watched the elderly Hispanic man hobble along on his cane. His esposa helped him by letting him support himself with a hand on her shoulder. She made the mistake of carrying a purse tucked under one arm.

Jack stepped down from his horse. He smiled, "I will take that purse, senora. It looks too heavy for you to carry." A barraged of bullets emerged from a side alley. Jack and Leon were cut to pieces by the slugs that hammered their bodies. When the gunsmoke cleared the two hated gang members were dead, bleeding from numerous bullet holes.

A shriek went up from the terrified onlookers. The old man and woman were also dead. Shot down by incidental gunfire. Hector walked out to examine the gringos. He motioned to the four other killers, "Come here. We need to tie them to their horses and send them back to Buster Mathis. Carlos will be pleased." Hector than toed the old man and woman checking them for life. He grinned as he bent down to pick up the bloodied purse, "I will take this. You no longer need it."

One of his men flung open the batwing doors of the Buckhorn and rushed inside. He shouted at Buster, "It's Jack and Leon. Their horses just toted them in, tied over their saddles. They've been shot all to hell!" Carlos exclaimed, "It's those damn Mexicans! Carlos Lopez will pay for this!" His man responded, "It's them alright. There was a Mexican peso tied to their bodies!" That further infuriated Buster, "If Lopez wants to have a pissing contest, we'll see who gets the wettest!"

Buster sent for Sheriff Martin, "Are you the Sheriff in this damn town or not?" Martin replied, "Of course I am. You was there the day I got elected!" Buster spit, "You can get unelected as easily as you got elected! Remember what happened to the old sheriff?...Do you get my drift?" The Sheriff nodded, "Yes, sir. What seems to be the problem?" Buster exploded, "What's the problem? What's the problem? Didn't you see my men tied across their horses? Murdered in cold blood?" Martin nodded again, "I saw em. I just figured they got tangled up in something they wasn't supposed to be in."

Buster began kicking over tables and chairs. Even the hard core drinkers headed out the door. Buster screamed, "Sheriff Martin, you get you posse together! I want you to wipe out Carlos Lopez and his bunch! Shoot em, knife em or string em up! It don't make me no nevermind! I want Mexican blood running in the streets!...If you can't handle that, you best leave San Antonio as fast as you can and pray I don't find you!"

Sheriff Martin deputized 20 men. He instructed them, "We're going into the Mexican part of town to kill Carlos Lopez and his gang." One of the new deputies asked, "How do we know who the gang members are?" The Sheriff retorted, "If you see a Mexican that looks suspicious, shoot him! We'll let God sort em out."

That day became infamous as Black Monday. Many people, white and Mexican lost their lives that day.

The posse fired randomly as they rode. Mexicans were shot down indiscriminately including men, women and children alike. It didn't take long before the Mexican population began to fight back. It wasn't just gang members, but the Mexican people as a whole. No one fights more fiercely than someone protecting their family.

Fifteen of the posse members were killed. Some were shot. Some were knifed. Others were beaten to death with clubs. Finally Sheriff Martin ordered the retreat, he shouted, "Back to our part of town!" The Sheriff had a broken arm due to a blow from a club from a Mexican woman. After he shot his attacker, Martin heard someone scream, "The bastards have killed Rosita!"

Buster sent a telegram to the Governor of Texas. When Buster got the reply declaring San Antonio to be under martial law and appointing Buster Mathis as the military commander, Buster shot Sheriff Martin though the heart. The bullet ironically penetrated the sheriff's badge. Buster smirked looking down at Martin's body, "As my first official act as military commander, it is my duty to inform you, Sheriff Martin, that you are fired!" Buster told the rest of his gang, "I hate incompetence...won't tolerate it!"

Buster wired the Governor back, thanking him for his expediency in the matter and refusing the Governor's offer to send troops. He told the Governor that he had the manpower to control the current unrest.

Manuel Sanchez sadly approached Burk as Burk was rocking in his chair on the porch. Manuel was a vaquero who had worked for the Four-Sixes for many years. Manuel was considered a top hand by Burk and Jake.

Manuel doffed his sombrero, "Senor Burk, I have bad news." Burk, Jake and Anne were alarmed. Manuel always had a smile on his face. Today he didn't. Burk responded, "Manuel, whatever it is, we can fix it!" Manuel replied, "I don't think so, Senor Burk. I must go to San Antonio. I am afraid my family is in trouble. I must see that they are safe."

Anne interjected, "Manuel, come in the house. I will fix you a cup of coffee...We may have some biscuits and bacon left over from breakfast." Manuel sighed, "Thank you, Senora, but I cannot eat...Maybe a cup of coffee would be nice." As they gathered around the table, Burk said, "When I was in town the other day, I heard there was trouble in San Antonio...something about a crooked sheriff."

When Manuel finished his coffee, he pushed back from the table, "I must go. My family needs me." Jake responded, "Let me get my things together. I believe I'll ride with you." Jake joked, "We can't have some other outfit hire you out from under us." Manuel smiled, "Thank you, Senor Jake, but I know what you're trying to do. I cannot ask you to put yourself in danger. You have your own family to look after."

Burk snorted, "Manuel, you are wasting your breath. I can see it in his eyes that Jake is going to San Antonio if he has to trail you!" Jake laughed, "Manuel, it wouldn't do for us to make a liar out of ol' Burk."

Manuel opened the door of the old shack. He called out, "Grandmother...Grandfather, where are you?" A curtain that was being used as a room divider was suddenly shoved aside. Manuel's sister, Maria launched herself into Manuel's arms. She sobbed uncontrollably, "Manuel, thank God you're here! Grandmother and

Grandfather are dead! They got in the way of the war between these gangs! Our little niece, Anna is also dead! These men have killed many trying to kill each other!"

Jake held his hat in his hands. Manuel introduced him, "Maria, this is my patron and friend, Jake Jackson." Jake asked, "Ma'am, I know this is a rough time, but what can you tell me about the gangs?" Maria sniffled, "It is two gangs. A gang of gringos led by a man named Buster Mathis. It is said that the Governor of Texas has appointed this man to be in charge of San Antonio. The other gang is Mexican outlaws led by Carlos Lopez. Both gangs are murderers. They have killed men, women and children."

Jake turned to leave. Manuel stated, "Wait, Senor Jake, I will go with you." Jake shook his head, "No, my friend, stay and take care of your sister and your neighbors. This is a job best done alone." Jake learned quickly that Buster Mathis could be found at the Buckhorn Saloon.

Jake pushed through the batwing doors and stepped to one side, allowing his eyes to adjust to the smoke and darkness. A man announced, "I need more men to ride against the Mexicans. I'm paying top dollar!" Jake walked over to Buster's table. Buster asked, "You have the look of a gunfighter. Do you want a job?" Jake grinned, "I already have a job." Buster responded, "And what would that be?" Jake's eyes narrowed, "Running you and your sorry bunch out of town."

There was a noticeable gasp from some of Buster's gang. Buster smirked, "Mister, you must be loco. The Governor hisself put me in charge here!" Jake shrugged, "That don't make me no nevermind. Burk Burnett is my partner. We know lots of folks in the Governor's office. I speck when the Governor finds out what's really going on here, you'll be relieved of your command...That's enough talk. I want you and your boys to leave San Antonio right now. Get to moving!"

Buster was livid. He was not used to being spoken to in that manner. Buster ordered, "Mister, you are loco!...Boys, kill him!" Buster and his three fastest gunslingers went for their guns.

The onlookers who observed the gunfight that became famous as The Shootout at the Buckhorn Saloon, were the balance of Buster's men, the bartender, several red-nosed bar flies and four saloon girls. They were shocked, then horrified. Down through the years whenever the bartender was asked how fast Jake Jackson was, he always gave the same answer, "I don't know. I never saw him draw."

Jake pulled his Colt and fanned the hammer four times. The .45 slugs opened up the bellies of all four outlaws. None of the outlaws cleared leather with their pistols. Buster and his henchmen crumpled to the quid-covered floor screaming from the pain in their stomachs. Buster begged, "Please, don't shoot no more! I hurt something fierce!"

Jake checked the crowd to see if anyone else was going to deal themselves in. When he saw there was no one, he calmly answered Buster, "Didn't plan on doing any more shooting."

Jake drew his skinning knife from the scabbard in the small of his back. With four quick swipes, he scalped the dying outlaws.

When he threw the bloody scalps on the bar, there was a stampede for the door. The remaining gang members were elbowing each other to get to the outside first. It was said that the rest of Buster's gang were last seen on galloping horses headed away from San Antonio.

Jake smiled at Manuel and Maria, "You needn't worry about ol' Buster and his gang. I think they disbanded today...permanently." Manuel shook Jake's hand, "Thank you, Senor Jake. I can never repay you!" Jake replied, "Don't thank me yet. There's still more work to do...Where can I find Carlos Lopez?" Maria replied, "He and his men hang out at Rosita's Cantina down by the canal. Rosita is dead. No one goes in there anymore except the Lopez gang."

Jake had to make a public display of ridding San Antonio of Buster Mathis. Since he was in a position of authority, people needed proof that Buster Mathis was dead and wasn't coming back. This was not the case with Carlos Lopez and his men. Jake looked at them as a nest of rats that needed to be exterminated.

Without any warning Jake entered Rosita's with his Colt in his right hand and his knife in his left. By the time he was finished so were Carlos Lopez and his men. There were ten of the worst blights on the Mexican people lying dead on the dirt floor. Jake grabbed a filthy lantern and broke it against the side of the cantina. The old building immediately burst into flames. Later that day, a fiesta was held around the ashes of Rosita's Cantina.

Caleb Burk shouted, "Ma! Grandpa! Pa's coming!...He's got Manuel with him!" Caleb Burk asked, "Did you get em, Pa?" Jake smiled, "I got em, son."

The End

Made in the USA
Coppell, TX
07 June 2020